TOO MANY LEPRECHAUNS

For Natalie Babbitt—S. K.

To my son, Bret—D. A.

 SIMON & SCHUSTER BOOKS FOR YOUNG READERS

An imprint of Simon & Schuster Children's Publishing Division

1230 Avenue of the Americas, New York, New York 10020

Text copyright © 2007 by Stephen Krensky

Illustrations copyright © 2007 by Dan Andreasen

SIMON & SCHUSTER BOOKS FOR YOUNG READERS is a trademark of Simon & Schuster, Inc.

Book design by Daniel Roode

The text for this book is set in Golden Cockerel ITC Roman.

The illustrations for this book are rendered in oil on paper.

Manufactured in China

10 9 8 7 6 5 4 3 2 1

Library of Congress Cataloging-in-Publication Data

Krensky, Stephen.

Too many leprechauns: (or how that pot o' gold got to the end of the rainbow) / Stephen Krensky ;

illustrated by Dan Andreasen.—1st ed.

p. cm.

Summary: Finn O'Finnegan returns home after a year in Dublin, and when he finds his village taken over by leprechauns, he must devise a way to get them to leave without making them angry.

ISBN-13: 978-0-689-85112-4

ISBN-10: 0-689-85112-X

[1. Leprechauns—Fiction. 2. Ireland—Fiction.] I. Andreasen, Dan, ill. II. Title.

PZ7.K883Too 2007

[E]—dc22   2005020659

first
edition

TOO MANY
LEPRECHAUNS

Or How That Pot o' Gold Got
to the End of the Rainbow

STEPHEN KRENSKY

ILLUSTRATED BY DAN ANDREASEN

Simon & Schuster Books for Young Readers

New York London Toronto Sydney

inn O'Finnegan looked like a rogue and walked like a rascal, so it was widely thought that he was at least one or the other. And his shadow, which followed him closely and knew all of his secrets, might have said he was both.

But when Finn returned home to Dingle after a year in Dublin, he was only looking to rest his feet and grow fat on his mother's soda bread.

The village looked much as he had left it—the stone walls a bit wobbly, the houses leaning into the wind. And yet something was clearly amiss.

At his own house Finn was surprised to find his mother cleaning up broken dishes with a broom.

Mrs. O'Finnegan let out a great yawn. "So here you are, Finn. And it would be glorious to see you if only I could keep my eyes open. But the leprechauns are everywhere, making fairy shoes with that infernal tapping, and none of us have slept in weeks."

At that moment Finn heard a steady *tap-tap-tap* in the yard. He stepped outside to investigate.

In the garden a leprechaun named Dobb was hard at work.

Tap-tap-tap-tap-tap.

"Good day," said Finn.

Dobb scowled at him. "It's a busy day, to be sure. The more shoes I make for the fairies, the more gold I get. And nothing is more important than gold."

Now, Finn had some experience with leprechauns, and he chose his words carefully. "A wise outlook. If I'm not mistaken, though, you may have missed a stitch."

Dobb dropped his hammer. "Missed a stitch!" He wagged a finger at Finn. "Fancy yourself an expert, do you? Come with me!"

Dobb led the way to a second leprechaun named Wattle. He, too, was making shoes—a dainty pair with silk flowers lining the sides.

"What say you to these?" asked Dobb. "Has Wattle missed a stitch too?"

Finn rubbed his chin. "Well, his shoes are fine, assuming—assuming they'll only be worn in the dark."

"*In the dark?*" cried Wattle.

"Where no one could see them," Finn explained.

Both leprechauns turned a deep shade of red.

The next day Dobb dragged Finn

to three more leprechauns.

And to four more the day after that.

By week's end, Finn had seen shoes of every size and style. And for each fault, flaw, or defect that he mentioned, the angrier the leprechauns became.

"Leprechauns are sensitive," Finn observed to his mother.

"And greedy, too," she added. "But don't put my heart crossways by taking too many chances."

There was a knock at the door from Dobb.

"You're just in time for tea," said Finn.

Dobb snorted. "It's not tea I'm after. It's you. Follow me."

Dobb led the way to a field, where all of the leprechauns stood waiting. As Finn approached, they moved back slowly to reveal a great pile of gold.

"We hardly could have gained all of this," said Dobb, "if our shoes were not the finest of their kind."

"Impressive," said Finn. He could see that the leprechauns loved their gold dearly—so dearly that it just might be their undoing. "Perhaps," Finn went on, "if I saw all your shoes together, I might change my mind."

"Yes, yes," the leprechauns agreed. They were sure that would make all the difference.

"Tomorrow morning we will bring the shoes to the village square," they promised.

Finn nodded. "I'll be counting on it," he said.

A gray dawn greeted the leprechauns as they arrived with their carts, barrows, sacks, and bundles. The shoes were unpacked and laid out with care.

Soon everything was ready. But while the leprechauns were there, and the shoes were there, Finn was not.

The leprechauns waited and waited.

The sky cleared before Finn finally appeared.

"Sorry, I'm late," he said, although he didn't sound sorry at all.

Finn marched up and down the street. At some shoes he stopped to point in astonishment. "Ahhhh . . . hmmmm . . . ohhhhh . . ." At others he simply clapped in delight.

"A very impressive sight," he said finally. "I can see why you were proud of your treasure."

Dobb frowned. "*Were* proud?" he repeated. "Are we not still proud of our gold?"

"Well, you could be," said Finn, "if your gold hadn't suddenly disappeared."

The leprechauns turned pale. "*Disappeared?*" Such a thing was beyond imagining. Still, it might be best to make sure.

Empty. They found the field empty.

"It must be here somewhere," Dobb insisted.

The leprechauns looked everywhere—behind
hedges, under rocks, even in the trees.

All night and into the dawn they searched
through Dingle, their lanterns flickering like fireflies
in the darkness.

But it did them no good. All of their fairy gold,
every last coin and nugget, was gone.

In the morning, when the mist still lay heavy on the air, the leprechauns came pounding on Finn's door.

"What have you done with our gold?" Dobb demanded.

Finn shrugged. "All is not lost—only safely tucked away. I'll make you a bargain. If you promise to leave Dingle and never trouble us again, I'll return your gold."

It pained the leprechauns to admit defeat, but not as much as it would have hurt them to lose their gold forever.

Reluctantly they agreed to his terms.

"Then we'd best be moving along," said Finn, looking up at the clearing sky.

He led them back to the empty field. At that moment the sun came out, and a rainbow fell from the sky. And there, where the rainbow met the grass, a great pile of gold suddenly appeared.

The leprechauns stamped their feet. "You moved our gold to the end of a rainbow. And when the rainbow vanished, so did our gold."

"Indeed," said Finn. "For it is fairy gold, as you told me, and fairies often use rainbows to move their gold about."

"You tricked us!" said Dobb.

Finn held up a hand. "The rainbow is back, and so is your treasure. Take it in peace while the rainbow holds—and remember our bargain."

Finn then went home to his mother, who—after a good night's sleep—baked him more loaves of soda bread than even he could eat.

As for the leprechauns, they were heard grumbling at times about how Finn had outwitted them. Yet they were secretly pleased as well. For if the truth be told, they've kept their gold at the end of the rainbow ever since.

THE END